Beverly Billingsly Takes a Bow

ALEXANDER STADLER

SILVER WHISTLE

HARCOURT, INC.

San Diego   New York   London

www.HarcourtBooks.com

Silver Whistle is a trademark of Harcourt, Inc., registered in
the United States of America and/or other jurisdictions.

Library of Congress Cataloging-in-Publication Data
Stadler, Alexander.
Beverly Billingsly takes a bow/Alexander Stadler.
p. cm.
Summary: When she auditions for the school musical, Beverly is
too frightened to make a sound, but she ends up being very important
to the class's performance.
[1. Musicals—Fiction. 2. Auditions—Fiction. 3. Schools—Fiction.] I. Title.
PZ7.S77577Be 2003
[E]—dc21 2002004503
ISBN 0-15-216816-8

First edition
A C E G H F D B

Printed in Singapore

The illustrations in this book were done in gouache and ink on Bristol Board.
The display type was set in Bostonia.
. The text type was set in Bell.
Color separations by Bright Arts Ltd., Hong Kong
Printed and bound by Tien Wah Press, Singapore
This book was printed on totally chlorine-free Enso Stora Matte paper.
Production supervision by Sandra Grebenar and Wendi Taylor
Designed by Lydia D'moch

To my brother David for the start,
and my brother Daniel for the finish
—A. S.

For her birthday, Beverly Billingsly received a trunk full of costumes from her great-aunt Bethesda.

Her parents never knew who would show up at the dinner table—jungle explorer, mad scientist, or tropical bird. One night she was the queen of Mesopotamia.

"Did you know," asked Beverly, "that nobody in Mesopotamia eats peas? Especially not the queen."

Beverly had always wanted to be a paleontologist, but now she thought she might want to be an actress as well.

So, Beverly was thrilled when Mr. Harrington announced that her class would be doing a musical called *Stormy Weather*. Finally, a chance to appear onstage.

"There will be auditions on Friday during lunch," said Mr. Harrington.

At breakfast the next morning, Beverly asked her father if he had ever auditioned for a play.

"Of course," answered Mr. Billingsly. "I played the part of Phillipe when my French class performed *Phillipe's Dream.*"

"Wow," said Beverly. "Did you have a lot of lines?"

"Not exactly a lot," said Mr. Billingsly. "I said, *Bonne nuit,*' blew out a candle, and went to sleep."

"And then what happened?"

"Then the dream began," said Mr. Billingsly, sipping his coffee.

Beverly practiced "The Banana
Song" in bed,

at the dinner table,

and even in the tub.

On Friday morning, Beverly
was so excited she could scarcely
concentrate. Her toes kept tapping
all through the geography lesson.

Finally, the lunch bell rang and it was time for the auditions. Roland Elsie did a Mexican hat dance and cracked open a piñata. Harrison Tewks sang a duet with a puppet.

Shauna Eliot sang a jingle from a soap commercial and then performed the dying swan solo from *Swan Lake*.

Beverly wished that she had saved her banana from lunch.

Then came Lois Furth. She marched herself to the middle of the stage, smiled big, and launched into "Singin' in the Rain." Beverly was amazed. Lois seemed to have no fear at all.

Now it was Beverly's turn. She took a deep breath and straightened her bow. She looked out into the auditorium and counted twenty-seven faces. That made fifty-four eyes staring at her and waiting.

Beverly opened her mouth to sing but no sound came.
She took another breath and tried again. Nothing. Her
knees started to shake. Beverly stopped.

"I'm sorry Mr. Harrington," she said. "I don't think I
can do this today."

"That's all right, Beverly," he said. "That was a very
good try."

After school, Beverly and Oliver Shumacher made their usual walk home.

"How was the audition?" he asked.

"A total failure," Beverly groaned.

"That bad?" asked Oliver.

"Worse," said Beverly.

Beverly was in a bad mood all weekend.

On Monday at lunch, Mr. Harrington handed out the scripts. Lois Furth and Roland Elsie had the leads—The Thunder Queen and The Sun King. They had a big number to sing in the finale.

Beverly got two parts—The Wall and The Shrub.

At dinner, Beverly told her parents what had happened.

"…and I only have one line," she grumbled, *"Please stop kicking me."*

"You know, honey," said Mr. Billingsly, "There really are no small parts, only small actors. Whatever you do, you can always try to do it very well."

"You mean I could be the best shrub and the best wall ever?"

"Exactly," said Mr. Billingsly.

After dinner, Beverly spent an hour studying the stone wall and several of the more interesting shrubs in the backyard.

By the first rehearsal, Beverly had memorized her line and half of everyone else's.

A week later, she knew the entire play.

Beverly stayed after school to help Mrs. Teenauer build sets and make costumes.

She made a large banner to advertise the performance and had Mr. Harrington hang it in front of the school.

Oliver helped her make 200 cupcakes to sell at intermission.
"Are you nervous?" he asked.

"Not really," answered Beverly. "All I have to do is stand
very still until Bertram Nakashima kicks me. Then I say my
line and that's it."

But inside, Beverly wondered if it would all be as easy
as she expected.

On opening night, everybody backstage was noisy
and excited—except Lois, The Thunder Queen, who was
fidgeting with her cloud and peeking through the curtain.

"Are you feeling all right?" asked Beverly.

"I was just thinking about how many people there are out there," said Lois.

"Isn't it great?" said Beverly. "Everyone's here. Oliver told me we already sold all two hundred cupcakes."

"Oh," said Lois. "Two hundred? That sounds like a lot."

Soon the theater was full and it was time for the show to begin.

Beverly took a last look in the mirror. She began to feel heavy and indestructible, as though she were actually made of stone.

When Bertram Nakashima kicked her, she called out in a deep, commanding voice, "Please stop kicking me." Bertram let out a little gasp and stopped.

Beverly changed into her shrub costume and came back onstage for the finale. She noticed that Lois's lower lip was trembling.

The band played the introduction, but Lois didn't sing.

"Lois!" Beverly whispered from behind her shrub, "Are you okay?"

Lois didn't move. She just stood there with a frozen smile.

Beverly thought fast.

"With a rattle and a boom...," she whispered to Lois.

"*With a rattle and a boom...,*" Lois repeated.

"I'll shake the moon...," said Beverly, as softly as she could.

"*I'll shake the moon!*" sang Lois.

Lois's smile unfroze as the words came back to her. Her voice got louder with each line and stronger with each note. When she and Roland came to the end of their duet, the crowd went wild.

As the class walked forward to take their bow, Lois turned smiling to Beverly and mouthed the words "thank you."

Beverly smiled back. She closed her eyes and listened to the applause. It was one of the nicest things she had ever heard.